Written by Janet Foxley

Illustrated by Pedro Bascon

Collins

Chapter 1

"*Two* cakes?" said Ruby-Rose in surprise, as her mother took a second tin out of the oven.

"This one's for Grandma," said her mother. "She's not very well, so I'm making her some tasty treats. I've got to go to work in an hour, so you'll have to take them to her on your own."

Ruby-Rose's mother put the cakes near the window to cool, and Ruby-Rose helped her to quickly make soup from vegetables and chicken leftovers. By the time the soup was ready the cakes were cool. They poured the soup into a jar with a tightly fitting screw-top and put one of the cakes into a tin with a lid.

3

"Now you *must* be sure to go round by the *road* today," Mother said, as she packed the treats into a basket. "Whatever you do don't take the short cut through the forest."

"Why not?" asked Ruby-Rose. The short cut was much quicker.

"Well, because of the … hunt." Her mother sounded as if it was something she didn't really want to talk about.

Ruby-Rose laughed. "The hunters won't mistake me for a deer or a rabbit – deer and rabbits don't wear red hats!" Ruby-Rose was very fond of hats. She was also very fond of red. She had a red hat for every occasion.

"They're not just hunting deer and rabbits, Ruby-Rose. They're looking for the girl who came round selling clothes-pegs last week. And the boy who'd just started working with me at the inn. They both went into the forest and simply disappeared."

"Oh, they were strangers round here," said Ruby-Rose. "I expect they just got lost."

"The hunters have been searching for days," said her mother, "but all they've found is their shoes. Please promise me that you'll ..."

"All right, all right," Ruby-Rose agreed impatiently.
"I won't go through the forest."

Because it was a warm, sunny day, Ruby-Rose chose
the red hat with the wide shady brim. Then she picked
up the basket and kissed her mother goodbye.

It was a *very* warm, sunny day and the basket was heavy.
By the time she got to the beginning of the path through
the forest, Ruby-Rose was already feeling tired.

She put her basket down for a few moments to rest
her arms. *I really don't want to go all the way round
by the road*, she thought. *It's so much further.
Mother always worries too much. I know
the forest paths very well. I'm not going to get lost.*

She picked up her basket and set off down the path through the forest, quite forgetting what her mother had said about the hunters finding the girl's and boy's shoes.

Chapter 2

At first, Ruby-Rose was happy that she'd come this way.
It was cool under the trees. Sunlight filtered through
the branches and birds were singing. But as she went
further, things changed. The trees closed over her head,
casting shadows so deep that she could hardly see
where she was treading. The birds fell silent. Now all she
could hear were her own footsteps. And other, softer,
footsteps.

r own footsteps, echoing back off the trees,
rself firmly. But she still kept turning round
re that no one was following her.

st cool, now. It was cold. *I wish I'd worn
red bobble hat instead of this sunhat*,
thought, as a shiver ran down her back.

Then Ruby-Rose turned a corner and saw a welcome pool of light ahead. She forgot how heavy her basket was and ran out into the sunshine.

Years ago someone had cut down some trees here and built a cottage. It was a ruin now, but its garden was still here and flowers bloomed bravely among the weeds. Ruby-Rose sat down happily on a pile of stones to rest and get warm.

"Mmmm!" growled a voice nearby.
"Something smells very tasty."

Ruby-Rose jumped up with a shriek. Someone *had*
been following her! She looked all round but couldn't
see anyone. Then something moved in the trees
and she could just make out the shape of a man.
A tall man with a cap pulled down over his face and
a heavy stick in his hand. A hunter!

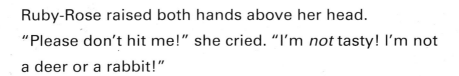

Ruby-Rose raised both hands above her head. "Please don't hit me!" she cried. "I'm *not* tasty! I'm not a deer or a rabbit!"

The man chuckled. "Oh, my dear young lady, I wouldn't dream of hitting you. This is just a walking stick. Now tell me what you've got in your basket that smells so tasty."

"Oh! In my *basket!*" Ruby-Rose's voice wobbled with relief. How silly of her to think he'd meant *she* smelt tasty! "It's soup and a cake for my grandma, because she's not very well."

"Dear me, I hope she gets better soon. But that basket looks heavy. Have you got to carry it a long way?"

"Not far now."

"So where does your grandma live, exactly?"

Why does he want to know that? thought Ruby-Rose.
Perhaps he's going to offer to carry the basket.
But before she could answer there was a sudden
shout followed by a loud crash close by.

"What was that?" The man raised his stick.

"Just a wood-cutter," said Ruby-Rose, "warning people to get out of the way of a falling tree. I expect we'll see his horse drag the log out on to the path in a minute."

"Can't stop," the man said hurriedly and before he'd even finished speaking he'd disappeared, not along the path but deep into the forest.

How odd, thought Ruby-Rose. *I wonder why he doesn't use the path*?

Ruby-Rose stayed in the clearing long enough to pick
a bunch of flowers from the old garden, then she set
off along the path again herself. Although it soon grew
dark again under the trees, the scent of the flowers
kept reminding her of the sunny clearing. But she
couldn't smell the soup and cake, in their jar and tin
with the lids tightly closed. *That man must have
a great sense of smell*, she thought.

Soon Ruby-Rose came to the place where the path divided. One way led straight to Grandma's cottage, but the other went deeper into the forest. *Perhaps this is where that boy and girl got lost*, she thought. But she knew which way to go, so she wasn't worried.

Then a figure stepped out from the trees right in front of her, blocking her path.

Chapter 3

"Ah!" gasped Ruby-Rose. She dropped her basket and backed hurriedly away. The figure had his back to what little light there was under the trees so she could only make out a dark shape.

"Careful, my dear," growled a familiar voice. "You don't want to spill Grandma's soup or crumble her cake."

"Oh, it's you again," said Ruby-Rose. "You scared me."

"Still afraid I might mistake you for a deer or a rabbit? You needn't worry, my dear. It's not deer or rabbits that I'm after."

"Oh," said Ruby-Rose. "So you're out looking for that girl and boy?"

"Who?"

"The children who got lost in the forest last week."

"Ah, yes, you're right. I'm looking for children." He took a step closer to her.

Ruby-Rose backed away. "What do you think has happened to them?" she asked, with a sudden wobble in her voice.

"I expect they've knocked on some cottage door, cold and hungry, and a kind person has taken them in and looked after them. Your grandma, perhaps. I must go and ask her. Why don't I come with you?"

The man picked up her basket and walked right up
to her, smiling. His teeth, Ruby-Rose noticed, were
surprisingly large and disgustingly yellow.
But the most unpleasant thing about him was
the *musty smell*. She snatched the basket from him
and backed further away.

Luckily the soup hadn't spilled and the cake hadn't
crumbled. But the flowers had fallen out of the basket,
which had tipped over, crushing them.

"Oh dear," said the man. "Your pretty flowers have got spoilt. But never mind, there are lots of wild bluebells just here, you can easily pick your grandma some of – oh! What was *that*?"

He's very jumpy, thought Ruby-Rose. *Every ordinary forest noise seems to scare him*. All she could hear was distant barking.

"Just dogs," she said. "I expect they're helping with the hunt."

"Dogs?" The man glanced nervously over his shoulder. "What are they hunting for?"

"The lost children, same as you."

"Oh, of course. Look, I've just remembered something urgent I have to do. I'll talk to your grandma another time. Where does she live?"

"Just down there." Relieved that he wasn't going to be coming with her, Ruby-Rose was happy to point to the right path. "The first cottage you come to."

The man melted into the trees just as suddenly as he'd appeared.

I don't like the way he does that, thought Ruby-Rose.

It's not normal. He's scared of something – but what?

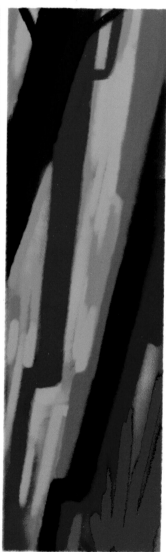

Ruby-Rose quickly picked a large bunch of bluebells, glad of their soft, sweet scent after the musty smell of the strange man. Then she ran the rest of the way to her grandma's cottage. She knew she would feel safe there.

Chapter 4

Grandma's cottage was usually cheerful and welcoming, but today it looked a mess. The flowers along the garden path had been flattened and the door had long scratches down it where paint was missing. It wasn't even shut properly, because it was so badly battered that the lock had fallen off.

What on earth has happened here? thought Ruby-Rose.
Anxiously she pushed the door open and went in.
The normally sunny cottage was as dark and chilly as
the forest. Something was wrong.

"Hallo Grandma! It's me! Are you all right?
What's happened to your door?"

"The wind," croaked Grandma, who was propped up in bed. "There was a terrible storm last night and the door was blown open."

"What a deep voice you've got today, Grandma," said Ruby-Rose in surprise.

"That's because of my sore throat."

"Mother's made you some soup. That should slip down your poor throat nicely. Are you hungry?"

"Oh yes, dear," growled Grandma. "Very hungry. Very hungry indeed."

Ruby-Rose unpacked her basket. "It's a lovely day, Grandma," she said. "Let me open the shutters. There's a musty smell in here. The fresh air and sunshine will make you feel better."

"No!" croaked Grandma. "Bright light will make my headache worse. Just sit here and let me look at you, my dear."

"But you can't *see* me, Grandma! It's so dark. *Please* let me open a window."

"Just one, then. But you mustn't open the shutters, because of my headache."

Ruby-Rose opened the window nearest the bed and gulped down mouthfuls of fresh air. A ray of light burst through the slats in the shutter and shone straight into Grandma's eyes. She put up a hand to cover them, but not before Ruby-Rose had seen them, brown and gleaming hungrily.

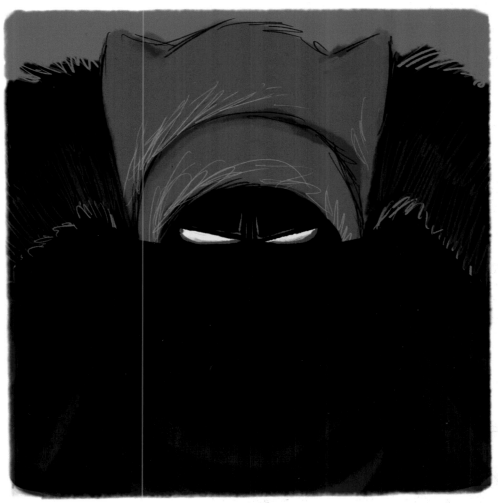

"What big eyes you've got, Grandma!" she said, surprised again.

"All the better to see you with, my dear." Grandma quickly spread out her fingers to cover the rest of her face.

"And what long nails you've got, Grandma! You must let me cut them for you. They look more like ..."

She stopped, staring in horror at Grandma's hand. Grandma's dark, furry hand.

"Claws?" said a voice that no longer sounded like
a sick old woman. "They do, don't they, my dear?
Very like claws." The figure leapt out of bed.
It wasn't Grandma. It wasn't even human.

"All the better to catch you with!"
said the wolf.

Chapter 5

"Don't touch me!" screamed Ruby-Rose, as she recognised the voice and the smell. No wonder she'd thought the man in the forest was a bit strange – he hadn't been a man at all! He'd been a wolf in a man's suit. And now he was a wolf in Grandma's nightdress!

"But I've come for dinner," he said, "and you, my dear, *are* dinner!"

Ruby-Rose kicked a chair over and dodged behind it, grabbing the first thing she could find to defend herself with – a big heavy stick that she also recognised. "What have you done with Grandma?" she demanded.

"Oh, I just locked her in the wardrobe. She was in the way." The wolf licked his lips. "And now it's time for my dinner. You look every bit as delicious and juicy as the girl and boy I caught last week."

Ruby-Rose gasped. So that's what had happened to them!
But now she needed to think quickly. The wolf was
between her and the wardrobe. She couldn't rescue
Grandma yet. She needed to rescue herself first.
"I may be delicious," she said, "but I'm very small,
not much of a dinner for such a big, fine wolf.
Why don't you start with Grandma's soup and cake?"

The wolf smiled his yellow smile and patted his stomach.
"What a kind, thoughtful girl you are," he said as he sat
down at the table. "Don't bother warming the soup.
I don't like hot food."

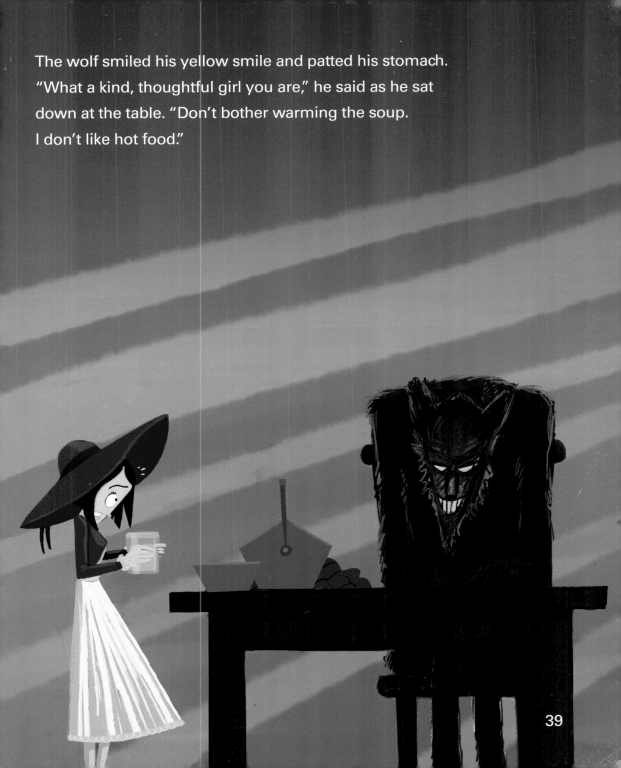

Ruby-Rose emptied the jar of soup into a bowl.
Then she secretly added all the salt from Grandma's
big salt jar. *Don't like hot food?* she thought, and she
tipped the contents of Grandma's pepper-pot into it too.
She gave the soup a quick stir and put it down
in front of the wolf.

He sniffed. "Chicken – my favourite! Delicious."
He picked up the bowl, poured the soup into his mouth
and swallowed it in a single gulp.

"PTHER! UGH! AAUGH!" The wolf started to cough
and splutter. Tears poured from his bulging eyes.

"Water!" he gasped, looking desperately around
the dark room. "Water!"

"Outside," said Ruby-Rose. "In the well."

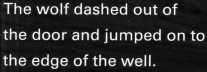

The wolf dashed out of
the door and jumped on to
the edge of the well.

He leaned down, frantically
trying to reach the water.

He leaned further.

And further.

And then Ruby-Rose crept
up behind him and pushed
him with both hands, as
hard as she could.

"*YOWOWOWL*!"

Ruby-Rose peered down
the well, but it was deep
and the wolf was already
out of sight.

Then she heard
a *KER-SPLASH*!

"Enjoy your drink!"
Ruby-Rose shouted.

She ran back indoors
and opened the shutters,
the windows and
the wardrobe.

Grandma was sitting on the wardrobe floor, huddled in her dressing-gown, gagged and bound with two of her own scarves. Ruby-Rose quickly undid them.

"Are you all right, Grandma?"

"I am now I've seen you safe, my dear. But what happened? What made that dreadful wolf run away?"

"He didn't seem to like his first course," said Ruby-Rose, "so he went for a long drink of water. I don't think he'll be back for the rest of his meal."

She helped Grandma to her rocking-chair and made her comfortable. "The soup's in the wolf," she said, "but we've still got Mother's lovely cake. Shall I make us a nice cup of tea?"

A map

happy

happy

hopeful

nervous